That's not my...
BIG colouring book

This book belongs to...

_____

 That's not my car.

That's my _ _ _ _ .

That's not my dog.

That's my ————.

That's not my
big dinosaur.

That's my
—— dinosaur.

That's not my duck.

That's my _ _ _ _ _

That's not my train.

That's my ———— .

That's not my
tall dinosaur.

That's my
_ _ _ _ _ dinosaur.

That's not my farmhouse.

That's my _____.

That's not my rabbit.

That's my ————————

That's not my plane.

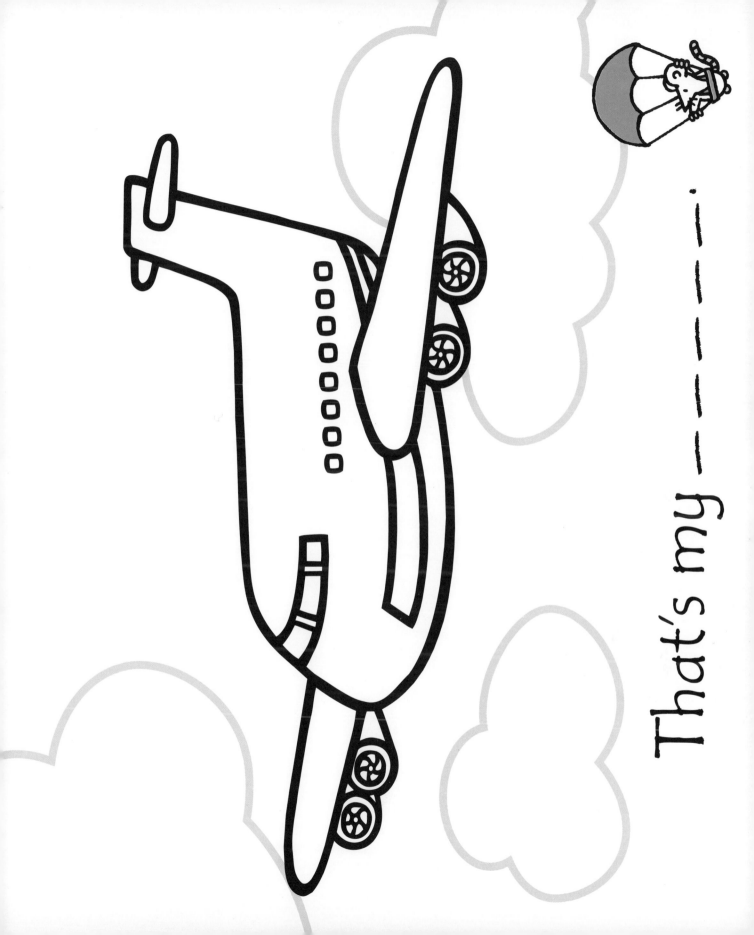

That's my – – – – – – – .

That's not my bumpy dinosaur.

That's my
————— dinosaur.

That's not my cat.

That's my ——————

That's not my
angry dinosaur.

That's my
_ _ _ _ _ _ _ dinosaur.

That's not my digger.

That's my _ _ _ _ _ _ _.

That's not my penguin.

That's my _____.

That's not my hen.

That's my _____.

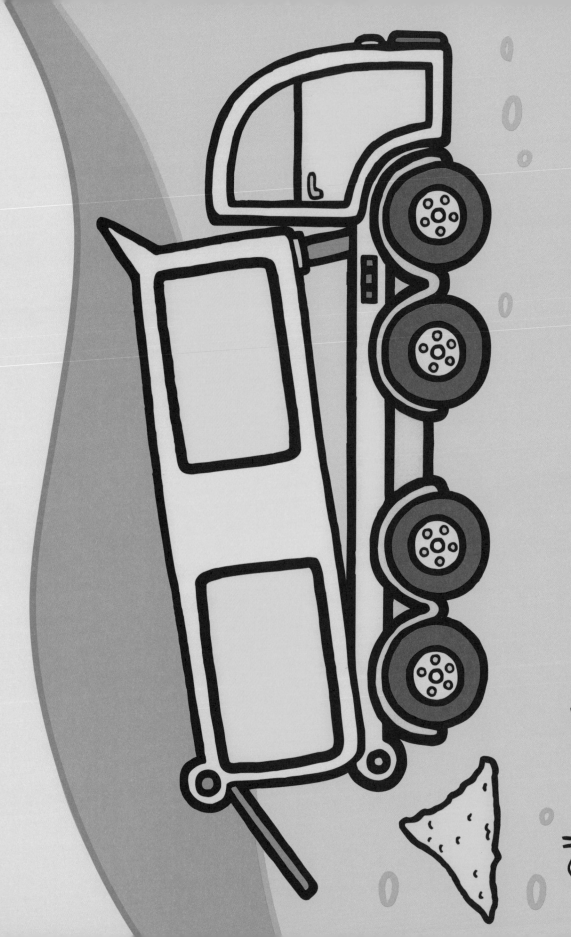

That's not my truck.

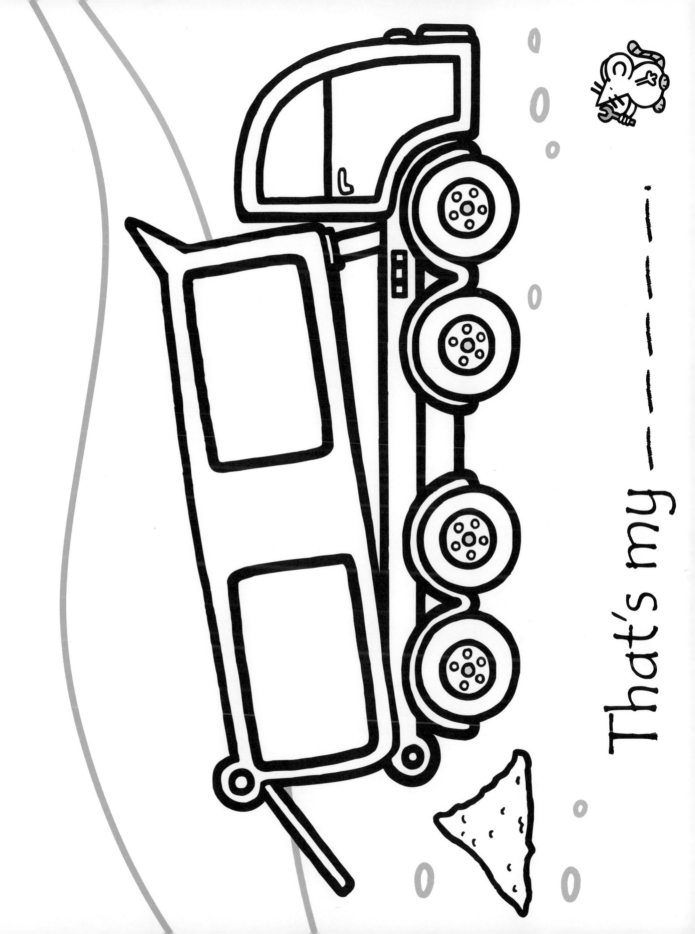

That's my _ _ _ _ _ _ _ .

 That's not my van.

That's my _____.

That's not my
long dinosaur.

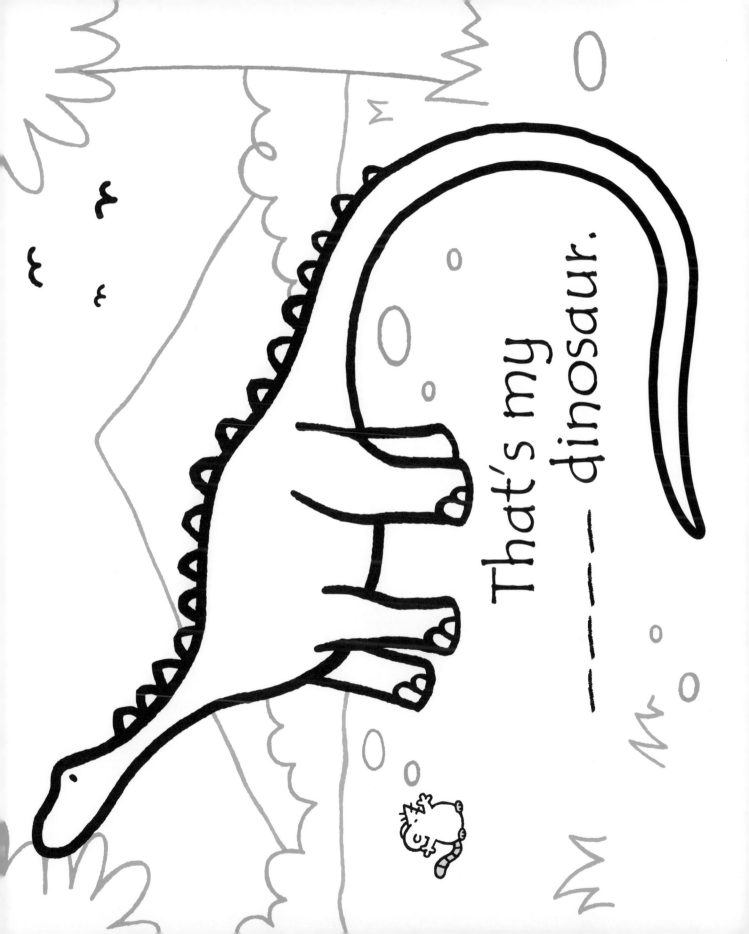

That's my
—— dinosaur.

That's not my cow.

That's my ____.

That's not my lion.

That's my _ _ _ _ _.

That's not my digger.

That's my _ _ _ _ _ _ _ _

That's not my fish.

That's my ----------

That's not my
large dinosaur.

That's my
———— dinosaur.

That's not my
scarecrow.

That's my

------- -------- --

That's not my goat.

That's my _ _ _ _

That's not my
scaly dinosaur.

That's my
————— dinosaur.

That's not my sheepdog.

That's my ˍˍˍˍˍˍˍˍˍ.

That's not my spotty dinosaur.

That's my ——— dinosaur.

That's not my
cockerel.

That's my

_ _ _ _ _ _ _ _ _ _ _.

That's not my spiky dinosaur.

That's my
—————— dinosaur.

That's not my kangaroo.

That's my _____.

That's not my swimming
dinosaur.

That's my _____
dinosaur.

That's not my sheep.

That's my _ _ _ _ _ _ .

That's not my elephant.

That's my _ _ _ _ _ _ _

That's not my panda.

That's my _____.

That's not my tractor.

That's my _____.

That's not my
noisy dinosaur.

That's my
———— dinosaur.

That's not my
lumpy dinosaur.

That's my
—— —— —— dinosaur.

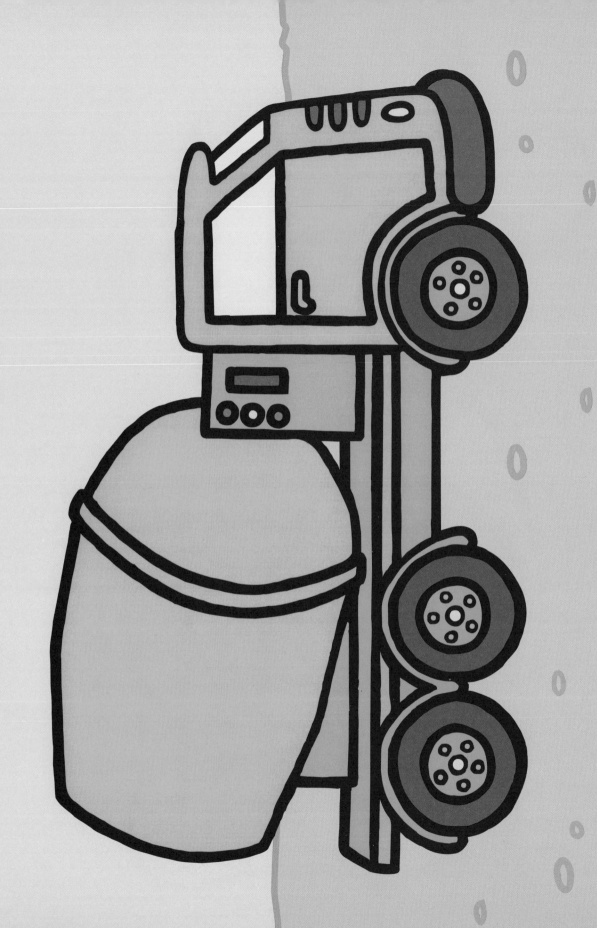

That's not my mixer.

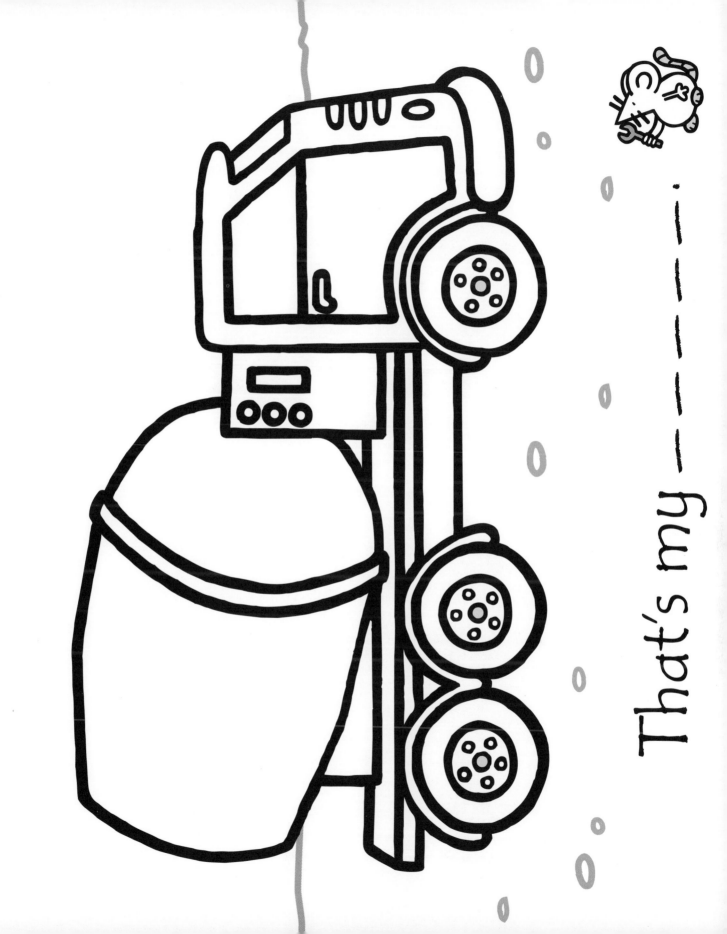

That's my _ _ _ _ _ _ _ _

That's not my horse.

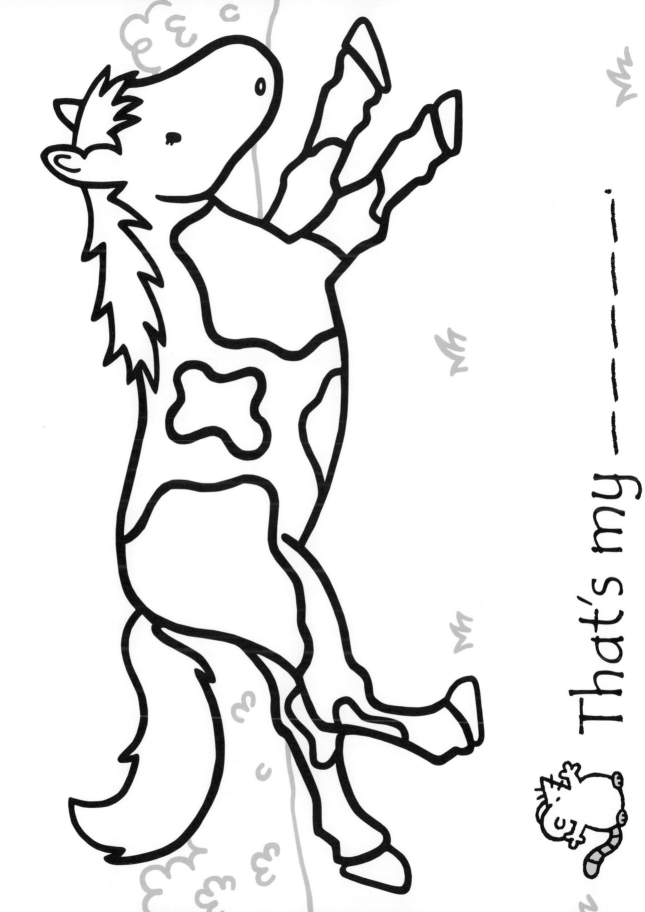

That's my _ _ _ _ _ _ _

That's not my
fat dinosaur.

That's my
—— dinosaur.

That's not my pig.

That's my ___ ___.

 That's not my bus.

That's my _ _ _ _.

That's not my tiger.

That's my _ _ _ _ _ _.

That's not my barn.

That's my _ _ _ _

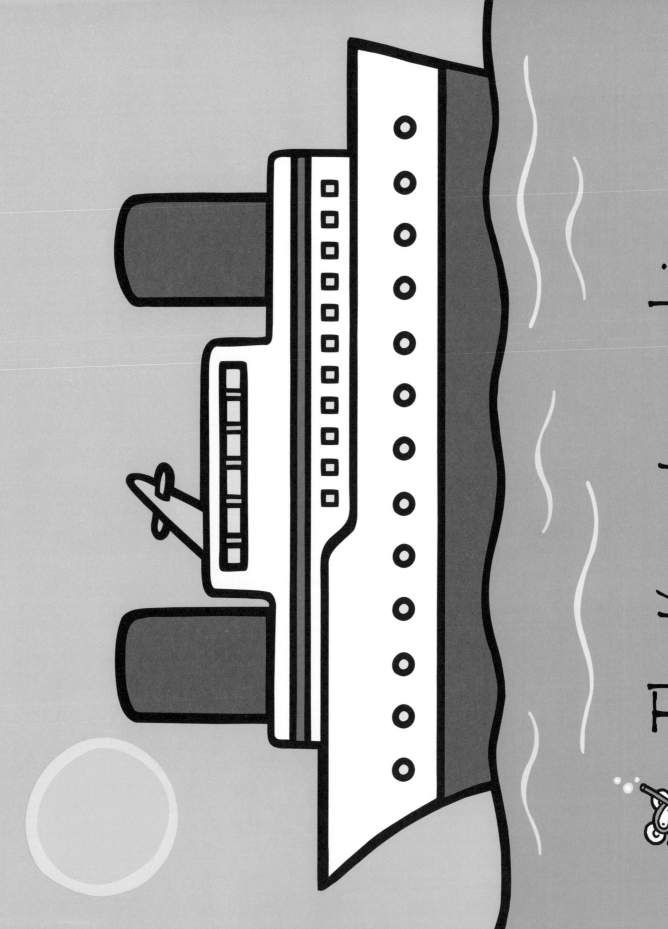

That's not my ship.

That's my _ _ _ _.

Animals

Things that go

Dinosaurs